GOOD GIRL.

GRA

ER!

This book is to be returned on or before
the last date stamped below.

1-3

FICTION

READING COLLECTION

LIBREX

REA
F
OFF

Falkirk Council

For Lydia

PUFFIN BOOKS

Published by the Penguin Group
Penguin Books Ltd, 27 Wrights Lane, London W8 5TZ, England
Penguin Books USA Inc., 375 Hudson Street, New York, New York 10014, USA
Penguin Books Australia Ltd, Ringwood, Victoria, Australia
Penguin Books Canada Ltd, 10 Alcorn Avenue, Toronto, Ontario, Canada M4V 3B2
Penguin Books (NZ) Ltd, 182–190 Wairau Road, Auckland 10, New Zealand

Penguin Books Ltd, Registered Offices: Harmondsworth, Middlesex, England

First published by Hamish Hamilton Ltd 1995
Published in Puffin Books 1997
1 3 5 7 9 10 8 6 4 2

Copyright © Hilda Offen, 1995
All rights reserved

The moral right of the author/illustrator has been asserted

Made and printed in Italy by Printers srl – Trento

GOOD GIRL, GRACIE GROWLER!

Hilda Offen

PUFFIN BOOKS

"Meet your new brother, Gracie!" said Mrs Growler.
"His name's Tommy."
"Would you like to give him a present?" asked Mr Growler.
"Yes," said Gracie. "He can have my rabbit."

Mr and Mrs Growler loved their baby.

"See how tiny his toes are!" said Mr Growler.

"Careful, Gracie!" said Mrs Growler. "You're treading on Tommy's rattle."

The Growlers watched the baby all the time.
"What dear little whiskers he has!" said Mrs Growler.
"Oh – look!" said Mr Growler. "He's smiling! It's his
very first smile!"

One morning the baby stopped smiling and started to cry.
He howled and howled and howled.
"We'll take him for a walk," said Mrs Growler.

"Look at me!" called Gracie.
"Ssh!" said Mrs Growler. "Tommy's quietening
down – you'll start him off again."

Suddenly the baby opened his mouth as wide as he could.
"He's trying to show us something!" said Mr Growler.

"It's his first tooth!" cried Mrs Growler. "Tommy's got his first tooth!"
"What a clever little chap!" said Mr Growler.

Not long after this Grandma Growler came to visit.
"Look what I can do, Gran!" said Gracie.
"Very nice, dear!" said Gran. "Now – where's my best boy?"

"He's over there," said Gracie.

"Tommy!" called Gran. "Give your old Grandma a cuddle!"

She hugged the baby and kissed him on the nose.

"Come in and have a cup of tea," said Mr Growler.
Grandma put Tommy down on the carpet.
"He's so sweet!" she said.

All at once the baby shot forward.
"Just look at that!" said Mr Growler. "Our Tommy's learned to crawl!"
"Well done, Tommy!" they said. "You clever, *clever* boy!"

People were always calling round to see the baby.
One summer's day Mr and Mrs Lion strolled up
the garden path.

"Auntie Rose! Uncle Joe!" called Gracie. "See what I've learned to do!"
"Good for you, Gracie!" they said. "Where's your little brother? We've brought him a jump-suit."

The Lions watched while Mrs Growler dressed the
baby in his new outfit.
"What a handsome child!" said Mrs Lion.
Tommy stood up. He lifted one foot – then another –

"Would you believe it?" cried Mrs Growler.
"Our Tommy's learned to walk!"
Everyone started to clap.
"Hip-hip-hooray!" they shouted.

While they were clapping and cheering the baby
opened his mouth.
"He spoke!" gasped Mrs Growler. "Tommy spoke!
I think he said 'Mum'."

"No, dearest, he said 'Dad'," said Mr Growler.
"I thought he said 'Auntie Rose'," said Auntie Rose.
"It was definitely 'Uncle Joe'," said Uncle Joe.
But Gracie heard what Tommy really said.

She jumped on her bike and rode away down the street
to the park. There was a lot to do before she could go home!

As she cycled back through the gate the baby
shouted out loud.
This time everyone heard what he said.
There was no mistake about it!
"GRACIE!" yelled Baby Tommy.

The grown-ups stared in surprise.
"Gracie walks on walls!" shouted the baby. "Gracie walks
on clothes-lines! Gracie rides upside-down on bikes!
Gracie does tricks on swings!"

"Well I never!" said Mr Growler. "Can you really do all those things, Gracie?"
"GRACIE RESCUED MY RABBIT!" roared the baby.

"Good heavens!" said Mr and Mrs Growler.
They gave Gracie a great big hug.
"You clever thing!" they said. "You good, *good* girl!
Well done!"

"Gracie! Gracie!" shouted the baby. "I want Gracie!"
Gracie took his hand.
"Come on, Tommy," she said. "I'll teach you
how to walk on a wall!"